The Small
Good Wolf

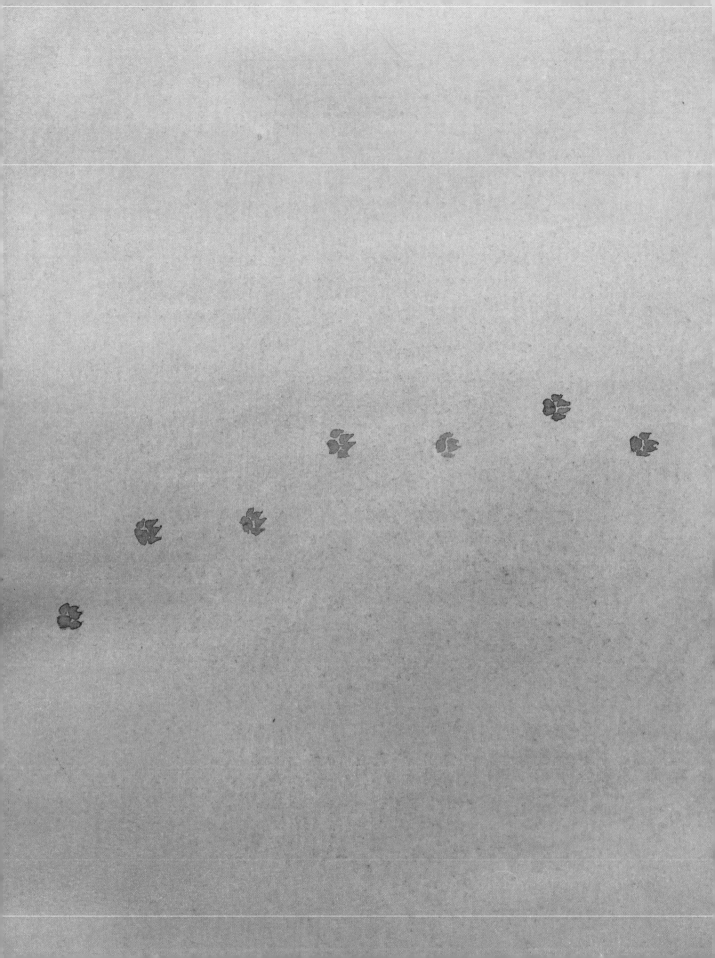

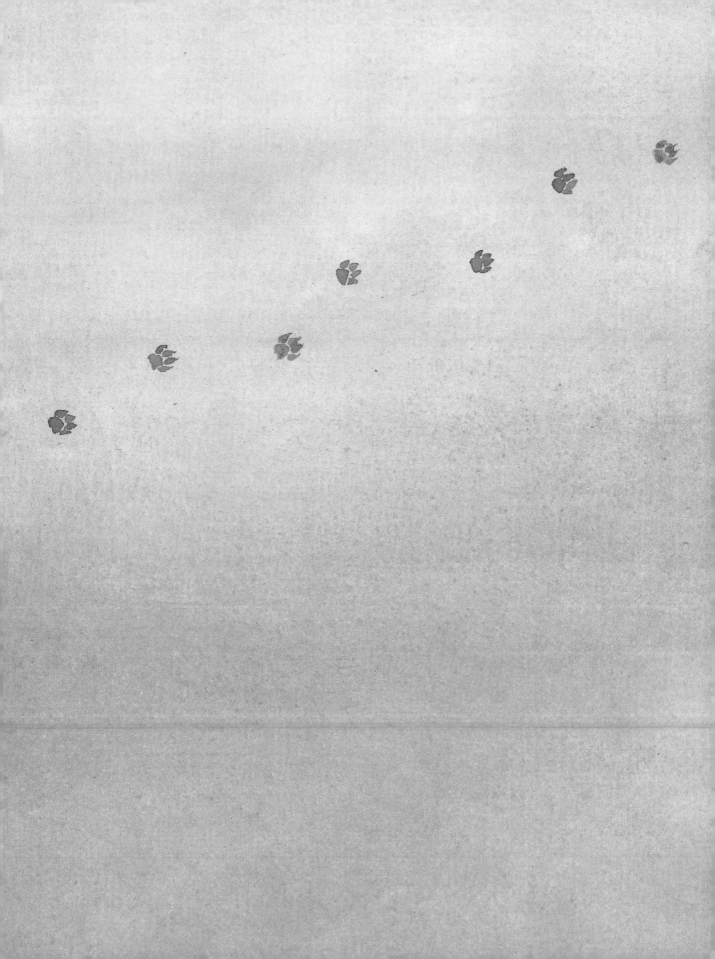

For the species *Canis lupus*

Also by Mary Rayner
Mr and Mrs Pig's Evening Out
Garth Pig and the Icecream Lady
Mrs Pig's Bulk Buy
One by One
Ten Pink Piglets
Wicked William
Mrs Pig Gets Cross

Text and illustrations copyright © Mary Rayner 1997

This edition published in 1997 by
Macmillan Children's Books
a division of Macmillan Publishers Ltd,
25 Eccleston Place, London SW1W 9FF
Associated companies worldwide

ISBN 0 333 65305 X (hardback)
ISBN 0 333 65306 8 (paperback)

1 3 5 7 9 8 6 4 2

A CIP catalogue record for this book is available from the British Library

Printed in Hong Kong

The Small Good Wolf

Mary Rayner

MACMILLAN CHILDREN'S BOOKS

Mother and father wolves tell this story to their cubs when they are in the cave, when snow has fallen and food is hard to find.

They tell it as a warning.

There was once a small good wolf. One morning, he was
out for a walk in the woods when he saw a human coming
towards him. Keep away from them, he'd been told, but he
was not only small, he was brave as well, so he did not run
away, he sat down and waited.

The human was old and mean. She threw a stone at him.
The wolf ran behind a tree.

Then the big bad human walked back along the path to her cottage, and the small good wolf came out from behind his tree and followed her. He thought there might be some food there.

She went inside and shut the door. He sat down under a tree. After a while, smoke came up out of the cottage chimney, and after some more time the old woman came out with some washing, which she hung on the line. Then she went in again.

I'll wait, thought the wolf. He was hungry, and still hoped there might be some food. Soon the old woman came out again. The wolf lay very still. She looked up the forest path, and then she said, "Drat the child, I'm not waiting around any longer," and she mounted her bicycle and rode away.

The small good wolf hoped she might come back, but she didn't. A long way off he could hear the sound of an axe, a woodcutter was working in the forest.

The wind made the clothes on the line flap. Then it blew some off. The small good wolf ran after them.

He felt with his nose if they were dry. They were. I'll take them in for her, he thought, then she'll be nice to me. So he carried them in his mouth to the cottage, and pushed open the door with his nose.

The cottage was warm. There was a bed in one corner, and a fire in the grate with a big washpot hanging over it, and on the wall there was a large mirror.

The small good wolf thought it would be fun to try on the clothes, so he put them on, and was just admiring himself in the mirror . . .

. . when there was a *rat-a-tat-tat* on the door. Help, he thought, where can I hide? So he jumped into the bed and hid under the bedclothes.

The door was pushed open and in walked *another* human.
The small good wolf shut his eyes and hardly dared breathe.
Footsteps came towards the bed.

Then they stopped. He opened one eye and looked. She was holding a basket with some food in it, a loaf of bread and some eggs.

"Oh Grandma," she said. "What big eyes you have!"

What a nutter, thought the small good wolf, doesn't she know a wolf when she sees one? But he thought, this must be some kind of game. I'd better play too, or something nasty might happen to me.

So he opened both eyes wide, sat up, and said, "All the better to see with, my dear."

"Oh Grandma," she said. "What a long nose you have!"

"All the better to smell with, my dear," said the small
good wolf, sniffing hopefully at the food in the basket. But
she didn't give him any.

Mean too, he thought, and he put out his tongue and
licked his lips.

"Oh Grandma," said Little Red Riding Hood, for it
was she. "What big teeth you have!"

Blow this for a lark, thought the small
good wolf, so he said, "All the better to
eat with, my dear," and jumped out of
bed to get at the food in the basket.

Little Red Riding Hood screamed,
and dropped it, and backed
across the room.

The woodcutter happened to be passing on his way home.
He heard, and rushed in with his big axe.

The small good wolf dodged, seized the basket in his teeth and ran out of the door.

The woodcutter comforted Red Riding Hood. "Where is that naughty old woman, your Grandma?" he said. "She should have waited in for you."

Just then there was a scrunch of wheels on the gravel outside, and the old woman came home. When she heard what had happened, she felt bad. But she didn't say sorry.

She said, "If anybody hears what really happened, they will blame me. So we'll make sure they don't. We'll say it was the wolf who was bad, won't we?"

The small good wolf ran home to his cave with the basket of
eggs and bread and shared it with his brother and sisters, and
they were very pleased.

The wicked old grandmother scalded herself doing the washing the very next week, and serve her right too.

But Little Red Riding Hood and her family, and her children, and their children's children, have been telling the story in their own big bad way ever since, and that is how you will have heard it. But if you were a wolf . . .

. . . you'd know different.

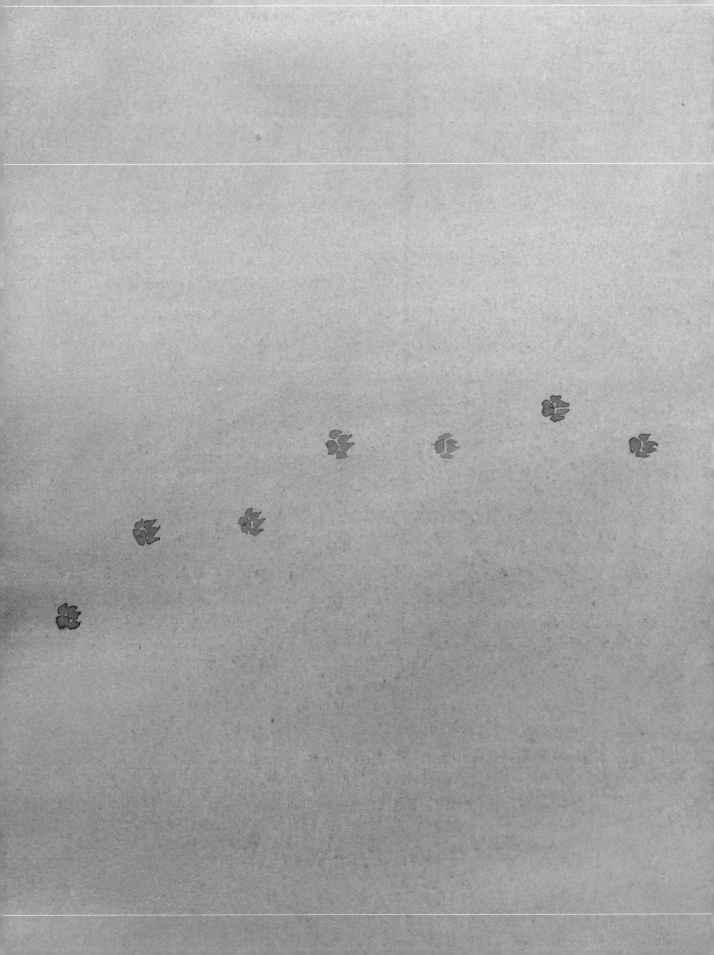

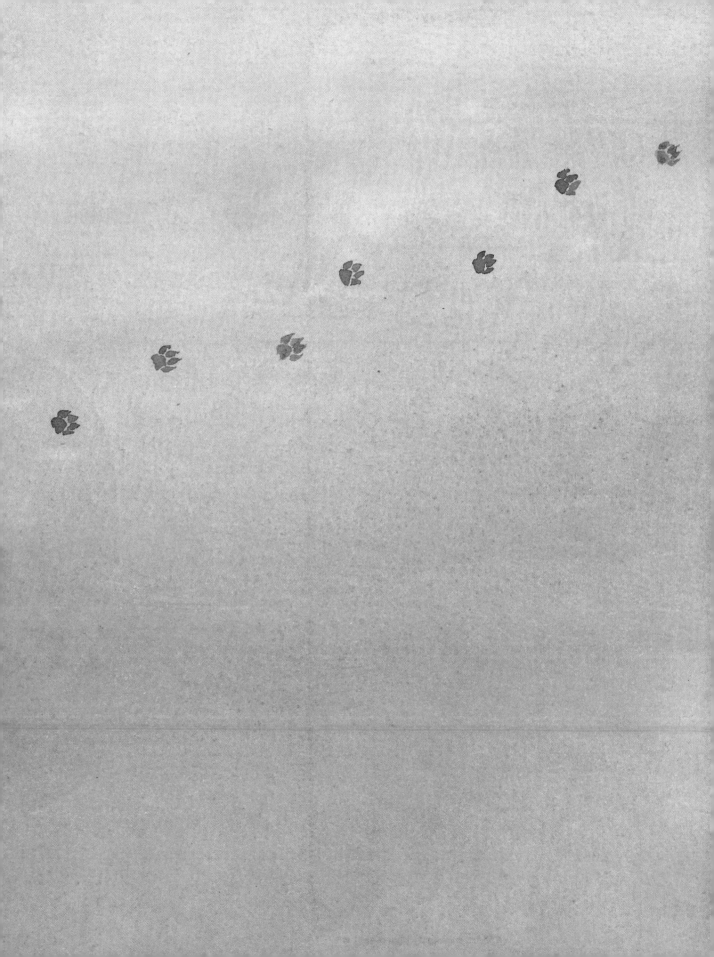